WHITNEY SOLVES A DILEMMA WITH SOLOMON

and learns the importance of honesty

THE EMERALD BIBLE COLLECTION

THERESE JOHNSON BORCHARD

ILLUSTRATIONS BY WENDY VANNEST

PAULIST PRESS
NEW YORK / MAHWAH, N.J.

Library of Congress Cataloging-in-Publication Data

Borchard, Therese Johnson.
    Whitney solves a dilemma with Solomon : and learns the importance of honesty / Therese Johnson Borchard ; illustrations by Wendy VanNest.
        p. cm.—(The Emerald Bible Collection)
    Summary: Having been transported by her emerald Bible back to the time of Solomon, ten-year-old Whitney helps him solve a dilemma and realizes that she must confess to cheating on a math test.
    ISBN 0-8091-6668-2 (alk. paper)
    1. Solomon, King of Israel—Juvenile fiction. [1. Solomon, King of Israel—Fiction. 2. Cheating—Fiction. 3. Honesty—Fiction. 4. Time travel—Fiction.] I. VanNest, Wendy, ill. II. Title. III. Series.

PZ7.B64775 Whi 1999
[Fic]—dc21   99-042582

Published by Paulist Press
997 Macarthur Boulevard
Mahwah, New Jersey 07430

www.paulistpress.com

Printed and bound in the United States of America

The Emerald Bible Collection
is dedicated
to the loving memory of
Whitney Bickham Johnson

TABLE OF CONTENTS

NANA'S EMERALD BIBLE

It was a warm August morning the day the Bickham family moved from their Michigan home to a residence in a western suburb of Chicago. Mr. Bickham's mother, Nana, who had lived with the family for some time, had passed away in February of that same year. Not long after, Mr. Bickham landed a great new job; however, it meant the whole family would have to leave everything that was familiar to them in Michigan and start again in Chicago.

It was especially hard on Whitney and Howard, the two Bickham children. They had grown accustomed to their school in Michigan and had several friends there. They didn't want to have to start over at a new school. Whitney, especially, was heartbroken about moving away from Michigan, for Nana's death alone had been very difficult on her. For Whitney, the Bickhams' Michigan home was filled with wonderful memories of Nana that she did not want to leave behind.

Nana and Whitney had had a very special friendship. Since Mrs. Bickham worked a day job that kept her very busy, it was Nana that had cared for Whitney from the time she was a baby. Growing up, Whitney spent endless hours with Nana. Her most wonderful memories of Nana centered around those afternoons when the two would go down to the basement and read stories from the Bible. Nana would sit on her favorite chair and read a story to

Whitney that related in some way to a problem Whitney was having. As Whitney sat on her grandma's lap listening to the story, her own situation always became a little clearer.

When Nana became sick and knew she was going to die, she called Whitney into her room and said:

"Dear Whitney, you know how special you are to me. I want you to have something that will always bring you home to me. I have a favorite possession that I'd like to leave with you—my Emerald Bible. Every time you open this special book, you will find yourself in another world—at a place far away from your own, and in a time way before your birth. But I will be right there with you."

Nana was so weak that she could barely go on, but, knowing the importance of her message, she pushed herself to say these last words:

"Whatever you do in the years

ahead, keep this Bible with you, as it will help you with all of life's most difficult lessons. And remember, when you open its pages, I am there with you."

As Nana closed her eyes to enter into an eternal sleep, Whitney spotted the beautiful Emerald Bible that lay at Nana's side. It sparkled like a massive jewel, and on its cover were engraved the words, "Lessons of Life."

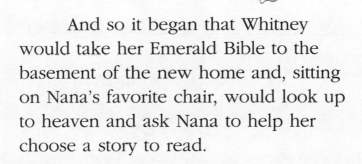

And so it began that Whitney would take her Emerald Bible to the basement of the new home and, sitting on Nana's favorite chair, would look up to heaven and ask Nana to help her choose a story to read.

CHAPTER ONE

MATH PROBLEMS

O ne month had already gone by since the day Whitney started at the new school in Chicago. She was doing fairly well in her new surroundings, especially given the recent death of her beloved grandmother, Nana. She began to laugh and play with her new friends—Tonya, Le Ly, and Maria—as she had done with Molly and Sue back in Michigan.

Whitney excelled in many subjects at school, especially English and history. She received A's

on almost all of her assignments in those classes. Math, however, was a different story. Not only was she bored by math, but she wasn't very good at it. Unlike English and history, both of which came easily to her, she would spend hours on her math assignments only to come up with the wrong answers.

Mrs. Bickham had suggested to Whitney that she get a tutor to help her with her assignments, but Whitney refused, promising her mother that she would ask Ms. Roberts and her friends for help. Whitney didn't have time for tutors. She wanted to spend all her free time on the soccer field.

"I am not going to spend any more time than I have to on boring math," she convinced herself.

One October day as Whitney set out for soccer practice, Mrs. Bickham asked her if she was done with her math homework.

"Ummm . . . yeah, Mom, almost," she responded, knowing full well that she hadn't even looked at it yet.

"Darn it! What do I do about that stupid assignment. I have to get to practice," Whitney thought to herself.

A lightbulb went off in her head. Maria had offered to help her with the assignment earlier in the day. Maria was quick at math and had already finished the assignment during the free period.

"You are not going to practice until your math is done," Mrs. Bickham yelled in the background.

Whitney was already five minutes

late for practice. She knew her coach would be mad if she showed up late. After all, there was a big game this coming weekend, and Whitney was one of the best players. He depended on her to score points.

She panicked. How would she get this assignment done in the next minute?

She came up with only one solution: to copy Maria's work. Maria had offered to help her. Why not copy the answers and go through the problems later? Whitney promised herself that she would look at the assignment after soccer practice. She would learn how to solve them later. But for the moment, she needed to get

16

to practice. And her mom was not going to let her go until she saw the answers jotted next to lots of scribble.

Whitney rushed to the phone to call Maria, hoping that she hadn't left for practice. Maria was usually running behind. The coach was less strict with her since she ended up sitting on the sidelines through most of the games anyway.

"Maria! I'm so glad you haven't left for practice yet!" Whitney said quietly so that her mom could not hear her discussion. "Listen, will you do me a favor and give me the answers for today's math assignment? My mom won't let me leave for practice until she sees that I am done. They will take me forever.

"I promise I will go through the problems when I get back," Whitney continued. "You can come over after

practice and we can go through them together, if that's OK."

"OK, sure," Maria said, not thinking about the consequences of sharing her answers with Whitney.

"Oh, thanks, Maria! You're the best!" Whitney said as she grabbed a piece of scrap paper from the kitchen drawer and a pencil to write with.

Maria went quickly through all the problems as Whitney recorded the answers. Whitney then transferred the answers onto a piece of paper full of scribble from last night's math problems.

"OK, Mom, I'm done," Whitney shouted as she jotted

down the last answer.

"Good for you!" Mrs. Bickham responded. "I'll see you after practice."

Practice went well as always for Whitney. She usually left the soccer field feeling confident, unlike in math class. Ironically, it was in math that Maria really shined.

The two decided after practice to make a deal: Maria would help Whitney with her math if Whitney would help Maria become a better soccer player.

The system worked well for a while,
until Whitney got lazy and started
copying Maria's homework instead of
learning how to do the problems
herself.

   Whitney's dishonesty and laziness
caught up with her one day in math
class. Because she hadn't been working
through any of the problems of her
assignments, she was unprepared for
the pop quiz Ms. Roberts
decided to give.
   Whitney began to
perspire as Ms. Roberts
passed out the tests. Five
minutes went by;
then fifteen; then
thirty. She
had not
answered
one single
question,
and the tests were to

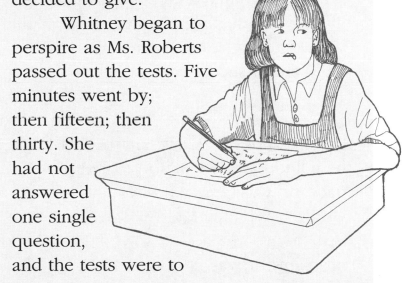

be turned in within the minute.

"What am I going to do?" she asked herself, panic-stricken at this point.

Whitney tried to get the attention of Maria, who sat in front of Whitney in class.

Whitney coughed quietly, so as to disrupt Maria, but not the teacher. There was no response. Whitney coughed a little louder.

Maria turned around to look at Whitney. Whitney's face was as pale as the moon. She was sweating through her clothes, as though she was in the middle of a soccer game.

Maria was somewhat annoyed. Sure, Whitney was teaching her a trick here and there about soccer, but the trade-off was becoming less and less worth it. Whitney had become dependent on Maria to solve her math problems. It was no longer Maria

tutoring Whitney; it was Whitney copying Maria's work. And Maria was getting tired of it.

Whitney could sense that Maria was reluctant to share her answers. But Whitney had no other alternative. She didn't have a clue as to how to solve the problems.

"Please!" Whitney whispered in desperation.

Maria did not want to be labeled a Goody Two-shoes. Being smart at math had already earned her the title of "math whiz," which she interpreted to mean "math nerd."

She leaned back in her chair so that Whitney could read the answers off her paper. Whitney quickly recorded them, relieved to have something written down on the blank piece of paper.

"Thanks!" she whispered when she had finished.

"OK . . . time is up!" Ms. Roberts said. She walked around and collected all the tests.

"Everyone sit tight until I have corrected your tests," Ms. Roberts continued.

Whitney had hoped Ms. Roberts would take the quizzes home with her. She didn't want to watch her correct and grade the tests. She was feeling bad enough as it was.

Five minutes went by. Maria did not turn around to talk to Whitney, as she often did when the class had free time.

Whitney knew that Maria was annoyed. She didn't know what to say.

"All right. You are all free to leave," Ms. Roberts said, dismissing the class for the day.

As everyone made their way to the classroom door, Ms. Roberts called Whitney and Maria back.

"Oh, no. Not you two. You are going to stay here," she said, reaching for each girl's elbow.

Whitney began to perspire again. And Maria grew more irritated. "No more of this deal," the math whiz thought to herself, convinced that learning to be a better soccer player was not worth the trouble that Whitney had gotten her into.

When the others had left the classroom, Ms. Roberts began her questioning.

"As I graded the exams, I noticed that you two had the same answers for each of the questions. And if everything

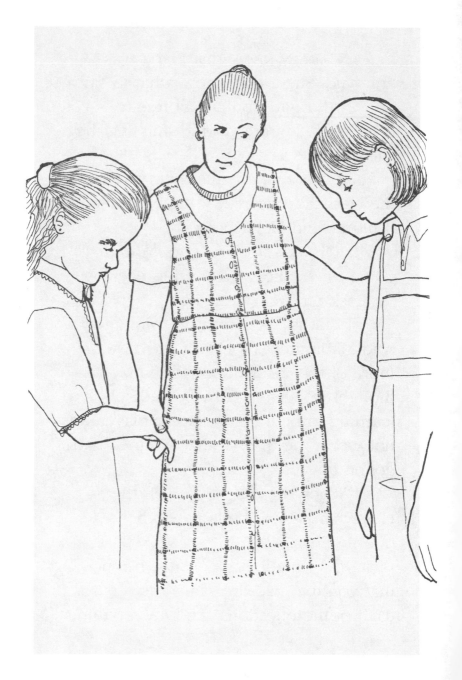

had been completely correct, I would not have suspected anything. However, one of the answers was wrong. And the equation that both of you used to come up with the wrong answer was identical. I don't think that is a coincidence, since you sit so closely to each other in class. Do you?"

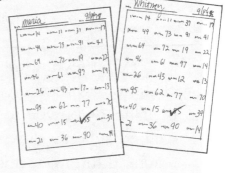

Whitney and Maria were silent.

Maria didn't think about this before giving Whitney her answers. Most of the time she scored perfectly on math exams. It would not have looked suspicious if she had done as well as she usually did. But this was a dead giveaway.

Before the two had a chance to respond to Ms. Robert's accusations, the teacher continued.

"I am afraid that I will have to fail

both of you if the person who is responsible for cheating does not come forward. I want both of you to go home and think about this. Report to me early tomorrow morning."

Whitney and Maria left the classroom without saying a word. With their heads bowed to the ground, they walked sullenly down the hall. Upon reaching the front door of the building, Maria turned to Whitney and said, "The deal is off. I no longer need your help with soccer."

Maria rushed out the door, making her way home.

Whitney continued walking at a pace no faster than a snail. She felt horrible. She thought

that the agreement she had with Maria would benefit them both. It had for a while.

"I really messed it up!" Whitney scolded herself.

All the way home she thought about what she should do, and what she should say to Ms. Roberts the next morning.

She looked up to heaven and cried, "Nana! Are you there? Can you hear me? I need your help!"

No one answered. There was just more silence.

As she opened the door to her town home, Bailey greeted her with a wet lick.

"Oh, Bailey, what have I done to deserve your wet licks each afternoon when I come back from school?" She bent down to pet her favorite pup in the whole world.

Bailey followed Whitney into the kitchen, where she looked inside the refrigerator to find something to eat.

"Yuck, nothing looks good. I have lost my appetite," she told her furry friend. Whitney was usually starving by the time she got back from school, but today she couldn't eat a thing.

"Maybe a movie will help," Whitney thought to herself, making her way down to the basement, where the

TV was. As she laid her backpack down, she saw something sparkling in the corner of the basement.

"Ah, the Emerald Bible. Surely one of Nana's stories would help me now," she said, beginning to feel a little better.

"Bailey, are you ready for another story?" she asked him. She thought back to the moment her grandmother gave her the precious Emerald Bible, and the words she said to Whitney just before dying: "Whatever you do in the years ahead, keep this Bible with you, as it will help you with all of life's most difficult lessons. And remember, when you open its pages, I am there with you."

Whitney picked up the beautiful book that sparkled as it had when it first lay by Nana's side. She went over to Nana's favorite chair and called Bailey, who plopped up onto her lap.

Whitney was quiet for a moment, preparing herself to leave the world she knew and enter into the one of the Old Testament, where the stories of Jonah, Joseph, and David had taken her. She was ready to visit the time before the birth of Christ, the place that was then called Canaan.

After a long, deep breath, Whitney looked up to heaven and said, "Nana, read me a story this afternoon. Choose a story of wisdom for me."

Rays of light emerged as Whitney gently opened the emerald cover. She thumbed through its delicate pages until her eyes stopped at a certain paragraph. She began to read aloud . . .

"Two women came to King Solomon and stood before him. The one woman said, 'Please, my lord, this woman and I live in the same house, and I gave birth while she was in the house. Then on the third day after I gave birth, this woman also gave birth. We were together; there was no one else with us in the house.'"

CHAPTER TWO

THE COURT OF SOLOMON

When Whitney looked up from the text, she found herself in a magnificent palace, seated on a royal throne, next to what looked like a king.

"Could I be the princess in this story?" she asked herself, studying her new surroundings.

The building in which she sat was truly marvelous. It was grand and elegant, like the Pharaoh's palace in Egypt, which she had visited with Joseph's brothers.

Although Whitney didn't know a thing about architecture, she knew that the design of this palace was the most

39

beautiful she had ever seen. Each room had been done with the utmost care and filled with the finest materials: brass, silver, and gold.

It was time for Whitney to play the detective and figure out where she was.

She looked around for clues. She noticed the word *Solomon* written on the back of the king's throne.

And she noticed many buildings surrounding the one she was in. The city was filled with temples and palaces. "It must be the capital of Canaan—the land that Joseph and David referred to in the other stories," she surmised, continuing her detective work.

"It sure looks as if this place is the hub of activity in this part of the world.

It must be one of the largest cities in Israel.

"Hmmm." Whitney thought back to the ancient map she had studied after reading the story of Joseph and his brothers.

"What is one of the largest cities in Israel?" Whitney asked herself.

"Jerusalem! That's it, Jerusalem!" Whitney had figured out her whereabouts without having to ask Solomon any questions.

But who in the world was she supposed to be? The court jester? Or was that in another time period?

Whitney was confused. Although

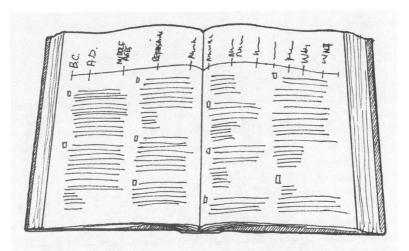

history was one of her stronger subjects in school, she had difficulty matching certain traditions and cultures to their proper periods.

Whitney had just begun to take in the grandeur of the palace when the king turned to her and asked, "What do you think I should do about this?"

Whitney felt as though she were back in Ms. Robert's class.

"Another pop quiz! Even in the land of the Bible. Unbelievable!" she thought to herself.

Whitney had been so busy

studying her surroundings that she hadn't even noticed the two women arguing about something in front of her. Apparently they wanted the king to settle their dispute.

"Would you both mind repeating your side of the story? In order to make a fair judgment, I must hear both sides again."

Whitney didn't have Maria in front of her this time to fill her in. She had to ask for more information.

"Thank you, Whitney. That would be helpful to me as well," Solomon said.

"Wait a minute," Whitney thought to herself. "When was I introduced to the king? How does Solomon know my name?"

She was baffled. But there was no time to figure this out. She needed to concentrate on what the women had to say so that she didn't flunk this pop quiz like the one she had flunked at school.

"I was just saying," the one started to explain as she pointed to the other woman, "that this woman here and myself were both pregnant at the same time. We were living in the same house when I gave birth. Then, three days later, she gave birth. There was no one in the house at this time but the two of us."

"Sounds simple," Whitney thought to herself. "I wonder where this is going."

"Then this woman's son died in the middle of the night," the first woman continued. "She got up from her sleep, came over to where I was sleeping with my son, and took him from beside me.

"She replaced my son with her dead son, so that when I awoke the next morning, I saw that my son was dead. However, as I looked at him more closely, I realized that it was her son that had died, not mine. The boy that

WHITNEY SOLVES A DILEMMA WITH SOLOMON

she laid down next to me was not my son."

"And I tell you," the other woman argued, "that the living son is mine, and the dead son is hers."

"That is not true," the first woman countered. "The dead son is yours; my son still lives."

The two women continued to argue before the court of Solomon.

"OK," Solomon interrupted. "We have heard what you both have to say."

THE EMERALD BIBLE COLLECTION

CHAPTER THREE

WHITNEY'S SOLUTION

Solomon called Whitney over to him. "How would you solve this dilemma, Whitney?" Solomon asked the young girl. "I need your help."

Whitney was flattered. She had never before been asked to help solve a mystery. This reminded her of a murder mystery game that she used to play with Sue and Molly back in Michigan. She hated to admit it, but it was a little like math. She had to come up with an equation that would lead her to the right answer.

Whitney thought back to her math quiz. She remembered what Ms. Roberts said about flunking both her and Maria if one of them didn't confess to cheating. She compared her situation at school to the case of the two women fighting over the baby.

"Hey! Maybe Solomon can do the same thing that Ms. Roberts did to find out the truth," she said proudly, as though, for the first time in her life, she had arrived at the right equation completely on her own.

Just as Ms. Roberts threatened to flunk both Whitney and Maria if the cheater didn't come forward, Solomon could say that he would kill the baby if the false mother didn't confess to her crime. Surely the true mother at that point would tell Solomon to keep the baby alive and give him to the other woman. That way, even if the real

mother couldn't raise him, she would save his life.

"I've got it, Solomon! I've got it!" she whispered anxiously into his ear. The two conferred quietly on the matter, and Solomon agreed that Whitney's plan was a good one.

"Brilliant!" he told her, impressed with her wisdom.

CHAPTER FOUR

THE TRUTH IS REVEALED

Solomon called everyone together. "Sir!" he shouted to one of his many servants. "Fetch me my sword."

The servant did as the king commanded.

"Yes, my lord," he replied obedicntly.

Solomon explained to the women how he would settle their dispute.

"Since both of you claim to be the mother of this boy," the king said with the mark of authority, "and the other son is no longer alive . . .

the only thing for me to do is to cut this child in half, so that each of you may have half of him."

Addressing the servant once more, Solomon shouted, "Divide the boy in two; then give half to one woman, and half to the other."

The plan was going as expected. As soon as the servant raised the sword to split the boy in half, the real mother came forward and begged, "Please, my lord, do not kill him. Give the other woman the living boy. She is his mother."

Whitney was right. The real mother, out of love for her

son, wished to save the child from death. She would rather live without him than see him killed.

Seeing true compassion in the eyes of the woman who spoke, Solomon ordered his servant to give the child to her.

"She is his mother," the king said, giving his final judgment on the matter.

CHAPTER FIVE

SOLOMON'S ORDER

After the two women left the court of Solomon, the king turned to Whitney and asked, "How did you ever come up with that solution? It was brilliant! Simply brilliant!"

Whitney didn't want to tell Solomon her situation at school. She didn't want him to think less of her for cheating, but there was no other way to explain how she came up with the solution.

"Well . . . you see . . . ," Whitney began to say, having trouble spitting out the words.

"At my school in Chicago," she

continued, "we study many subjects." Solomon wanted to interrupt her right there and ask her where in Canaan was the land of Chicago, and what she meant by a *school*. But seeing that she was already stuttering, he kept his questions to himself.

"One of the subjects that I am not so good at is math. To be completely honest, I hate it. So I made a deal with a friend of mine that I would help her to become a better soccer player if she helped me with math."

Solomon couldn't stand it anymore. It was as if this little girl was speaking a foreign language. In all of his wisdom, he could not figure out what she was talking about. It was unlike him to be confused, since he was the wisest man in Israel.

"Whitney," he interrupted. "Where is this land of Chicago that you speak about?" Solomon thought he knew every town in Canaan. But he had never heard of Chicago.

Whitney paused for a moment. She knew that Solomon was very wise; however, there was no way she could tell him about the United States without confusing him more. If Solomon didn't even know about Jesus, surely he wouldn't comprehend the Americas. Besides, she didn't have time to teach him the history of the world up to present times. And even if she did, would he believe her?

He was the king of Israel. She was a little girl from a land he hadn't heard of.

"It's . . . ahhh . . . it's not in Canaan," Whitney responded. That was the easiest way to answer his question. And he accepted it, since he wasn't in the mood for a geography lesson either.

"I'm sorry. Continue," Solomon said, apologizing for the interruption. He realized that Whitney's story wouldn't make complete sense to him since he didn't know the culture of the place from which she came. He had traveled enough in his life to understand that people in different lands do different things and have different customs.

Whitney continued her story.

"Anyway, I became lazy and started copying my friend's work instead of doing it myself. When the teacher gave us a pop quiz, I was totally unprepared. So I cheated and wrote down my friend's answers."

Solomon could finally see where Whitney was going with the story. Like the two women, each of whom claimed to be the mother of the living boy, Whitney and her friend both claimed credit for the answers on a math quiz.

"Interesting," Solomon remarked.

"So when the teacher realized that one of us had stolen the work of the other, she threatened to flunk both of us," Whitney continued.

"Yes, I see," Solomon interjected, fascinated by the story.

"And so . . . what happened then?" Solomon was waiting for the conclusion to the story. But Whitney didn't have one, since she had not yet resolved her situation.

"Well . . . ," Whitney responded, embarrassed to tell him that she hadn't yet come forward to confess her wrongdoing. "That is for tomorrow."

"You mean to say that you haven't yet confessed to stealing her work?"

Solomon asked. Whitney could hear the disappointment in his voice.

She was ashamed and bowed her head.

"Whitney, you must return to your land at once and resolve this situation. You must do the honorable thing. You must confess to cheating."

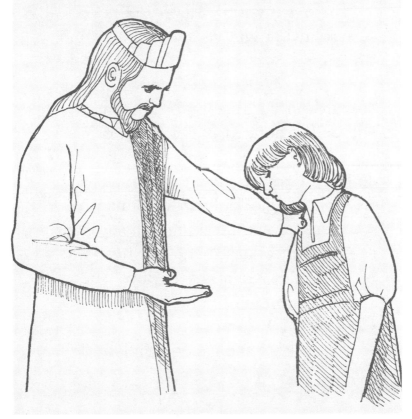

Solomon spoke with authority. In her storytelling, the ten-year-old forgot that she was in the presence of a king. And this king could command her to do anything he wished.

"Go to it!" he ordered her as he had ordered the servant to fetch his sword.

"Yes, my lord," she responded obediently. "I will go as soon as I find my pup."

Whitney had been concentrating so hard on the case before Solomon that she hadn't noticed Bailey roam off as the women argued. And the palace was so huge that she hadn't a clue as to where to begin looking for him. She wandered down the long hallway next to the courtroom, calling out his name.

"Bailey! Come here, pup!" she yelled, disrupting the next case that went before Solomon.

"Bailey!" she called a little more quietly.

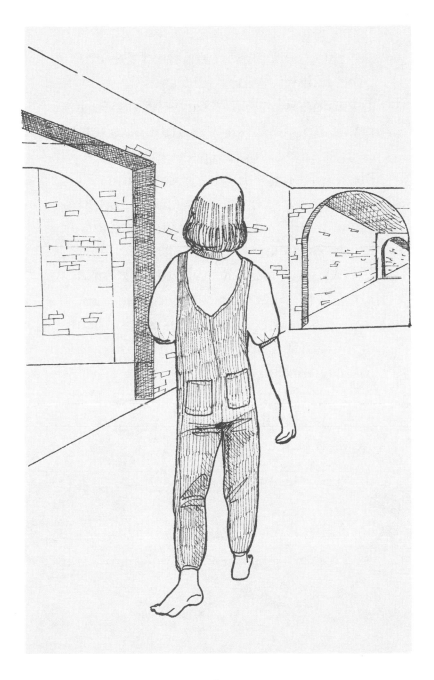

She had almost reached the end
of the hallway when she saw
something white and furry wrapped up
in what looked like a purple blanket.

"Bailey! There you are!" she said,
relieved to have finally found him.
However, as she walked closer to him,
she realized that he was wrapped up in
the king's robe.

"Uh oh. Bailey, where did you
find this blanket?" she asked her pup.
Bailey looked up with eyes so innocent
that Whitney couldn't dream of
scolding him.

"OK, then. We'll
just have to tell
Solomon his

66

robe is a little hairy," Whitney said, shaking off as much fur as possible from the velvet robe.

Whitney cleared her throat before reentering the room in which Solomon sat, now in the middle of another dispute.

"Excuse me, my lord." Whitney interrupted. "I have found my dog, so I will be leaving."

She had one more thing to say. "I do have a slight confession to make to you, as well," Whitney admitted. "Your robe seems to be covered in white dog hair."

Solomon laughed, which was a relief to Whitney.

"Thankfully the king has a sense of humor," she said to Bailey. "Now let's go home."

Whitney looked around for her Emerald Bible. It was not with her. She

panicked. This was the first time she had lost her Emerald Bible.

"Bailey, we can't leave this world until we find Nana's Bible! You must help me find it!"

It was Bailey's turn to reenter the courtroom of Solomon. He ran underneath the small throne that Whitney was sitting on earlier. Underneath the golden throne was the Bible. It was still bookmarked to the story of Solomon's judgment, waiting for Whitney to read the final paragraph.

Bailey picked up the book with his mouth and brought it to Whitney. She opened the Bible at the marked page and began to read the last paragraph aloud.

"All Israel heard of the judgment that the king had made; and they stood in awe of the king, because they knew God had given him the gift of wisdom."

CHAPTER SIX

A CONFESSION TO MAKE

As soon as Whitney looked up from reading the last paragraph of the story, she found herself once more seated on Nana's favorite chair with Bailey on her lap.

"We've got an order from the king, Bailey! We mustn't wait any longer!" Whitney was anxious to take her problem before the court of Ms. Roberts, just as the women in the Bible had taken their dispute before the court of Solomon.

She called up Maria to see if she had time to return to school to talk to Ms. Roberts. Whitney and the others knew that Ms. Roberts stayed at school until five o'clock each afternoon. The teacher told her students the first day of class that she would be available after school to talk privately about any problem. This was reassuring to Whitney since Mrs. Bickham usually didn't return home from work until dinnertime.

Maria was still annoyed with Whitney when she answered the phone.

"I really don't feel like talking about it," Maria said before Whitney could get a word in.

"Well, in that case, I will go to Ms. Roberts alone and tell her that it was I who cheated, and that you deserve an A."

"Really? You are really going to do that?" Maria perked up upon hearing this.

"Of course I am, Maria. You are my friend. You were only trying to help me, and I took advantage of that."

Whitney continued with her apology. "I'm sorry, Maria. I really am. Will you forgive me?" she asked her friend.

Maria was quiet for a moment and then responded, "Yes, Whitney. I can forgive you."

Like the mother in the story who saved the life of her child, Whitney felt as though she had just saved her friendship with Maria. She would never let her laziness get in the way of a friendship again. And she would be sure from now on to work through her own math problems so that she would be prepared for any pop quizzes.

"Whitney," Maria said before hanging up, "our deal is on again if you promise to do your own homework."

"That would be great, Maria!

I promise to do my part this time," Whitney replied.

As soon as she hung up the phone, Whitney fetched Bailey's leash and clipped it onto his collar. As she bent down to tie the shoelaces on her sneakers, she turned to her pup and said, "C'mon Bailey, we're late to appear before the court of Ms. Roberts."

THE EMERALD BIBLE
COLLECTION

Also in
THE EMERALD BIBLE COLLECTION

WHITNEY RIDES THE WHALE
WITH JONAH
and learns she can't run away

WHITNEY SEWS JOSEPH'S
MANY-COLORED COAT
and learns a lesson about jealousy

WHITNEY COACHES DAVID
ON FIGHTING GOLIATH
and learns to stand up for herself

ABOUT THE AUTHOR

Therese Johnson Borchard has always been inspired by the wisdom of the Bible's stories. As a young child, especially, she was intrigued by biblical characters and awed by their courage. She pursued her interest in religion and obtained a B.A. in religious studies from Saint Mary's College, Notre Dame, and an M.A. in theology from the University of Notre Dame. She has published various books and pamphlets in which she creatively retells the great stories of the Judeo-Christian tradition.

ABOUT THE ILLUSTRATOR

Wendy VanNest began drawing as a small, fidgety child seated beside her father at church. He gave her his bulletin to scribble on to help her keep still during the service. People around them began donating their bulletins, asking her for artwork, and at the end of the service, an usher would always give her his carnation boutonniere. As a result of this early encouragement, she pursued her interest and passion in art, and has been drawing ever since.